TWO MONSTERS

DAVID MCKEE

TWO MONSTERS

Mini Treasures

RED FOX

1 3 5 7 9 0 8 6 4 2

Text and illustrations © David McKee

David McKee has asserted his right under the Copyright,
Designs and Patents Act, 1988
to be identified as author and illustrator of this work

First published in the United Kingdom 1985 by Andersen Press Limited

First published in Mini Treasures edition 1997 by Red Fox
Random House, 20 Vauxhall Bridge Road, London, SW1V 2SA

Random House Australia (Pty) Ltd
20 Alfred Street, Milsons Point, Sydney,
New South Wales 2061, Australia

Random House New Zealand Ltd
18 Poland Road, Glenfield,
Auckland 10, New Zealand

Random House South Africa (Pty) Ltd
PO Box 2263, Rosebank 2121, South Africa

Random House UK Limited Reg No. 954009

A CIP catalogue record for this book
is available from the British Library

ISBN 0-09-922012-1

Printed in Singapore

To Carme Solé vendrell
and the mountain

There was once a monster that lived quietly on the west side of a mountain.

On the east side of the mountain
lived another monster.

Sometimes the monsters spoke together through a hole in the mountain.

But they never saw each other.

One evening the first monster called through the hole, "Can you see how beautiful it is? Day is departing."

"Day Departing?" called back the second
monster. "You mean night arriving, you twit!"

"Don't call me a twit, you dumbo, or I'll get angry," fumed the first monster and he felt so annoyed that he could hardly sleep.

The other monster felt just as irritated
and he slept very badly as well.

The next morning the first monster felt awful after such a bad night. He shouted through the hole, "Wake up, you numskull, night is leaving."

"Don't be stupid, you peabrain!" answered the second. "That is day arriving." And with that he picked up a stone and threw it over the mountain.

"Rotten shot, you fat ignoramous!" called the first monster as the stone missed him. He picked up a bigger stone and hurled it back.

That stone also missed. "Hopeless, you hairy, long-nosed nerk!" howled the second monster, and he threw back a rock which knocked the top off the mountain.

"You're just a stupid old wind-filled prune!" shouted the first monster as he heaved a boulder that knocked another piece off the mountain.

"And you're a bandy-legged, soggy cornflake!" replied the second monster. This time he kicked a huge rock just for a change.

As the day passed the rocks grew bigger and bigger and the insults grew longer and longer.

Both of the monsters remained untouched but the mountain was being knocked to pieces.

"You're a hairy, overstuffed, empty-headed, boss-eyed mess!" shouted the first monster as he threw yet another massive boulder.

"You're a pathetic, addlebrained, smelly, lily-livered custard tart!" screamed the second monster hurling a yet larger rock.

That rock finally smashed the last of the mountain and for the very first time the monsters saw each other.

This happened just at the
beginning of another sunset.

"Incredible," said the first monster putting the rock down he was holding. "There's night arriving. You were right."

"Amazing," gasped the second monster dropping his boulder. "You were right, it is day leaving."

They walked to the middle of the mess they
had made to watch the arrival of the night
and the departure of the day together.

"That was rather fun," giggled the first monster. "Yes, wasn't it," chuckled the second. "Pity about the mountain."

RED FOX
Mini Treasures

COLLECT THEM ALL!